ONCE SHE LOVED

ÂME LIBRE

HARMANPREET KAUR

ISBN 979-8-89984-637-3

Dedication

To the girl—

The one who kept quiet when her world shattered, The one who loved too deeply, broke too silently, And still stood back up, alone and trembling. This is for her. This is for you.

You made it through.

And to every soul reading this—

May you find pieces of your healing in these pages.

Contents

Part III: Flight (The Rise)

Part I: Ashes (The Fall)

Chapter 1

The Beloved Date

"Sometimes, we don't fall in love. We walk into it, hoping it will hold us—only to realize we stepped into a storm."

Before Samuel, Aaranya was learning how to breathe again.

Not laugh—not dream. Just breathe.

Her days were quiet rituals of healing: herbal tea steeped in silence, dog-eared books with highlighted hope, long walks that ended with sunsets she didn't photograph. She was building herself back, one careful layer at a time, after years of emotional erosion.

She had boundaries now. Walls. Rules.

Don't trust too quickly. Don't give too much. Don't romanticize apologies.

She had learned. The hard way.

But healing is not a straight line. And sometimes, the universe sends a test disguised as a miracle.

That miracle had a name—Samuel.

He came into her life like a whispered promise. Gentle at first. All soft words and soulful stares. He didn't ask much, only noticed things that others overlooked. The chipped nail polish on her left hand. The way she hugged with hesitation. The tears in her voice when she said, "I'm fine."

She wasn't fine. But she was functioning. Until Samuel made her feel again.

It started with laughter—real, unfiltered, belly laughter she hadn't known in years. Then, the conversations. Deep ones. About death, dreams, and things people only say at 2 a.m. And just like that, the girl who swore she'd never let anyone in again found herself lowering her guard.

One evening, under an orange sky, he looked at her like she was a prayer he forgot he needed. Then softly, dangerously, he said:

"Babe, I need a small favor… Can I borrow your pendant for a little while?"

That pendant—her father's last gift. A lifeline she wore close to her collarbone, like a memory stitched into skin.

Her lips said yes. Her soul whispered no.

But when you've been lonely long enough, even red flags look like fireworks.

That night, Aaranya gave away more than a pendant.

She gave away her safety.

Her story.

Her trust.

And still, she loved it.

Naively.

Fully.

Fatally.

Chapter 2
The Storm That Followed

"Sometimes, love doesn't sweep us off our feet. It crashes into us, like a wave we never saw coming. And we are left trying to breathe again."

After that first encounter with Samuel, Aaranya couldn't shake the feeling of unease. She had built walls around her heart after her past, walls so thick that nothing, not even the gentleness of a man like Samuel, could easily breach them. But Samuel wasn't someone to give up quickly. He persisted. Not with force, but with patience. He didn't push her to reveal too much about herself. He didn't demand answers to questions she wasn't ready to answer. He simply let her be—observing her with kindness, waiting for the day she would speak freely again.

Yet, with every soft smile he gave her, every polite inquiry about her well-being, Aaranya felt both drawn and repelled. She couldn't help but wonder if he was like the others—there to break her further, to extract the last pieces of her soul that still clung to hope. Or was he truly different? Was he calm after the storm?

Her days were spent with distractions, things that kept her mind from wandering to dangerous places. Work consumed her, as it always did. But it wasn't the work she wanted to talk about—it was the sudden reminder of a time before, when she had been vibrant, full of life. It was that version of herself she missed, the one she had lost when trust was shattered and her heart was left in tatters.

Yet, in the midst of all that inner chaos, Samuel remained there—a quiet observer, never judging, never pushing. And as the days turned into weeks, Aaranya found herself slowly lowering her guard, allowing small pieces of herself to slip past those walls she had built.

One afternoon, after another long day of work, Samuel called her.

"Aaranya," his voice was soft, his tone almost hesitant, "Would you like to meet? Just for a coffee? I promise no heavy conversations, just a few words between two people trying to get through their lives."

It was simple, innocent, and yet it struck her deeply. She hadn't realized how much she longed for simplicity until that moment.

After a brief pause, Aaranya finally agreed. "Okay, Samuel. I'll meet you."

When she arrived at the café, the scent of freshly brewed coffee filled the air, and the sound of soft conversations and clinking cups gave the place a welcoming warmth.

Samuel was already there, waiting for her at a corner table, his eyes scanning the room until they landed on her. The smile that broke across his face was enough to make her heart flutter, and for a moment, she felt like she could breathe again.

"*You made it,*" *he said, his voice warm, as he stood to greet her.*

She smiled back, though it didn't quite reach her eyes. The weight of her past still hung heavy on her chest, but she was trying to let herself feel something, even if it was just the tiniest flicker of hope.

They sat down, and as Samuel ordered for both of them, Aaranya couldn't help but feel the tension in the air between them. She wasn't sure what she expected from this meeting, but she knew one thing for sure—this was different.

For once, it wasn't just about the past. It wasn't about the mistakes and betrayals that had marked her life. It wasn't about the scars or the pain. For once, there was a space for something else to emerge—a possibility.

They spent hours talking about everything and nothing. The conversation flowed easily, like it had when they first met, but this time, it felt different. She felt like she could talk about things that mattered—her hopes, her dreams, her fears—but most of all, she found herself listening to him in a way she hadn't with anyone in a long time.

And when the evening came to an end, Samuel stood, offering her a gentle smile. "I hope you had a good time, Aaranya."

"I did," she admitted, feeling something stir inside her that had been dormant for so long.

"Take care of yourself," he said, his voice soft but steady.

As she walked away from the café, Aaranya couldn't help but wonder if this was the beginning of something more, something new. Or was it simply another distraction, another fleeting connection that would fade away as soon as it had arrived?

Only time would tell. But for the first time in a long time, she allowed herself to wonder what it might be like to feel something again.

Chapter 3
Unraveling Truths

"The moment you let someone in, you risk the chaos of vulnerability. But without it, you'll never know the peace that comes from being truly seen."

Days passed, and Aaranya found herself drawn to Samuel in ways she couldn't explain. The coffee had been the beginning, a simple act that sparked a chain of events she hadn't anticipated. She couldn't quite put her finger on it, but something about him made her feel like she was standing at the edge of a precipice, ready to leap into the unknown. The fear was still there, lingering at the back of her mind, but for the first time, she felt like it was worth confronting.

She began to look forward to their interactions. It wasn't just his patience that stood out, but the way he seemed to understand her silence, her reluctance, without needing her to explain it. Samuel gave her space, but he also made her feel like she wasn't alone.

One evening, after a long day, Aaranya was sitting on her couch when her phone buzzed. It was a text from Samuel.

"Hey, are you free tomorrow evening? I know a place with amazing views. Thought you might like it."

Aaranya hesitated. She had grown accustomed to the safety of her routine, to the solitude that allowed her to control every aspect of her life. But this was different. Samuel wasn't asking for much—just time.

"Okay," she replied. "Where are we going?"

"It's a surprise," he responded. "I'll pick you up at 7?"

She agreed, a mix of excitement and nerves swirling inside her. The next evening, as promised, Samuel showed up at her door. He was dressed casually but still managed to look effortlessly charming. Aaranya had to admit, there was something about him that made her feel both comfortable and restless at the same time.

They drove in silence for a while, the only sound was the hum of the car's engine. Aaranya stole glances at him, noticing the way his hands gripped the steering wheel, the focus in his eyes. There was a quiet intensity about him that she couldn't ignore.

Finally, they arrived at their destination—a small, secluded spot on the edge of the city, overlooking a sprawling valley. The view was breathtaking. The setting sun cast a warm golden glow over the landscape, and for a moment, Aaranya forgot to breathe.

Samuel got out of the car and walked around to open her door. His eyes met hers, and for the first time, she saw something deeper in them—something that made her heart skip a beat.

"This is beautiful," she murmured, stepping out of the car. The breeze was cool, and the evening sky was painted in shades of orange and pink.

"I'm glad you like it," Samuel said, his voice soft. He led her to a small bench overlooking the valley, and they sat in silence for a while, just watching the world unfold around them.

It was the kind of quiet that wasn't uncomfortable. It was the kind of silence that allowed for unspoken words to be shared, for emotions to settle in the space between them without needing to be verbalized.

But eventually, Aaranya couldn't help herself. She had to ask.

"Samuel... why are you doing this?" she asked, her voice barely above a whisper.

He looked at her, his expression unreadable for a moment before he answered, "Because I want to. Because I want to be here with you."

The simplicity of his answer caught her off guard. She had expected something more, something complex, but all he had given her was honesty. It was raw, and for some reason, it made her heart ache.

"I don't know what to make of all this," she confessed, her eyes on the horizon.

"I'm not asking you to," Samuel replied. "But I'm here, Aaranya. I'm not going anywhere."

His words settled in her chest, heavy and reassuring. She had built her walls high, and for good reason. But in this moment, with Samuel beside her, she was beginning to wonder if maybe, just maybe, there was a reason to let them down.

Later that evening, as they sat in the car, Samuel's hand brushed against hers. The contact was fleeting, but it sent a shockwave through her, making her heart race.

"I don't know if I'm ready for this," Aaranya admitted quietly, her voice filled with doubt. "I'm not sure I can trust again."

Samuel nodded, his expression softening. "You don't have to be ready. Not yet. Just take your time. But I need you to know… I'm here for the long haul. No pressure. Just… when you're ready."

The words hung in the air between them, and Aaranya felt a sense of warmth wash over her. It wasn't a promise of forever. It wasn't a guarantee of happiness. But it was something. It was the beginning of a possibility.

As Samuel drove her home that night, Aaranya realized something. She didn't have all the answers. She didn't know if she was ready to let her guard down completely. But what she did know was this: she was willing to try. For the first time in a long while, she was willing to take the risk. And perhaps, in that, she had already begun to heal.

Chapter 4

Echoes of the Past

"Some scars don't fade. They echo in silence, in smiles that don't reach the eyes, and in the hesitation before every step forward."

The days that followed weren't loud. They didn't explode with fireworks or declarations. Instead, they whispered—a gradual weaving of comfort and presence. Aaranya didn't speak of her past, not in full, but Samuel seemed to understand the weight she carried without her needing to spell it out.

It was a Tuesday afternoon when she heard a knock at her door. Not a message, not a call. A knock—real, physical, intrusive in a way that sent a chill down her spine.

She opened it slowly, only to see a man standing there with a calm confidence that felt both familiar and foreign.

"Aaranya?" he asked, his voice low but assured. "It's been a while."

She stared at him, confused. Then the pieces fell into place.

"Hudson?" Her voice cracked.

Her stepbrother. The name she hadn't spoken in years.

He looked different. Sharper, colder—like life had carved angles into him she hadn't remembered. A crisp formal shirt, expensive shoes, and an aura that screamed success. It was clear—he had done well for himself. She remembered vague mentions from relatives—senior financial analyst, some foreign projects, living far from home—but he had vanished from her world when she needed him the most.

"What are you doing here?" she asked, unsure whether to invite him in or shut the door entirely.

"I heard… about everything. The hospital, Mom, the house." His voice wavered for the first time. "I should've come sooner."

Aaranya took a step back. The silence between them wasn't healing. It was sharp. Raw. It held too many unanswered questions.

"I don't need apologies now, Hudson. I needed a presence back then."

He nodded, his eyes dark with something she couldn't quite name—regret, maybe. "I get that. I do. But if there's a way I can be part of your life again…"

She didn't reply. She couldn't. Not yet.

Just then, her phone buzzed. A text from Samuel:

"I'm outside. Thought you could use a walk."

Aaranya looked back at Hudson. "I need time. I'm not ready for this either."

He nodded and stepped away, letting her close the door.

She slipped into the passenger seat of Samuel's car. He didn't ask what had happened. He didn't press. Just drove.

And maybe that was what made her speak.

"My step brother came today," she said, eyes fixed on the passing road. "He left years ago. Didn't even come back when things fell apart."

Samuel stayed silent, letting her fill the silence with the pieces she'd never voiced.

"I hated him for a long time. I still do… sometimes. But seeing him—he looked like someone who had made peace with the past. I haven't."

Samuel's grip tightened on the steering wheel for just a second. "Healing doesn't always look graceful, Aaranya. Sometimes it's just… continuing."

They drove to the riverside, a place she hadn't been in years. The water shimmered under the fading sunlight, and the soft rustling of leaves felt like a lullaby to her weary thoughts.

Samuel sat beside her as she traced lines in the dirt with a stick, not speaking. He didn't need to fill the silence. That, more than anything, grounded her.

"You know," she said softly, "I spent so long trying to pretend none of it mattered. That I was fine. That I didn't need anyone."

Samuel leaned back, his arms resting behind him. "You don't need to be strong all the time. And you don't have to carry everything alone."

Aaranya looked at him, really looked. For the first time, she wondered—not what Samuel wanted from her—but what he had lost too

"What about you?" she asked. "Who did you have to become for the world?"

Samuel's jaw clenched slightly, a flicker of darkness crossing his eyes. "That's a story for another night."

And just like that, a balance was struck—two broken souls, quietly trying to rebuild without demanding answers, just offering presence.

Chapter 5

The House That Grief Built

"Grief doesn't knock. It moves in. Unpacks its bags. Rearrange your furniture. And sometimes, it answers the door before you do."

The house was quiet—too quiet. Aaranya had returned to her childhood home to gather some old documents, but the moment she stepped inside, the silence hit like a blow to the chest.

Dust danced in streaks of sunlight, and everything smelled faintly of naphthalene and memories. The living room hadn't changed much. The faded maroon sofa still sat against the wall, sagging a little more than before. The photo frames stared at her like ghosts—her mother's smile, her younger self, and one picture of Hudson, frozen in time beside them.

It was strange, how a place could feel like both comfort and punishment.

She moved slowly through the rooms, her fingers brushing old memories—furniture that once echoed laughter, shelves that once held dreams. Grief didn't just haunt these rooms. It lives here. It was stitched into the curtains, into the worn corners of the table where her mother used to sit with her tea.

In the bedroom, tucked in the drawer of her mother's wardrobe, she found the gold chain.

She held it in her palm, heart thudding. It had been her mother's. Not expensive, not flashy. Just… meaningful.

Aaranya sat on the bed, chain in hand, and allowed herself to cry—not loud, not wild. Just quiet tears, like soft apologies to a past she couldn't change.

The next morning, she walked into the kitchen and found Hudson at the stove.

"I figured we could at least have coffee," he said over his shoulder, trying to sound casual.

"You don't drink coffee," she replied, surprised.

"I do now," he smiled, handing her a cup.

She sat, taking a sip, watching him. "Why are you really here, Hudson?"

He leaned against the counter, the cup cradled between his hands. "I left when things got hard. I told myself I needed to focus on work, on success. And I got all that—a good job, financial security, respect. But when I saw your name on that hospital file… it shook me. I realized I was living in a world built on avoiding everything I didn't want to feel."

Aaranya studied with him. The suit, the smooth words, the composure—it all looked so polished. But underneath, she could see it. The cracks. The guilt.

"I don't need you to fix anything," she said. "But if you want to be here, be here. Stay through the hard stuff. Not just the coffee."

Hudson nodded. "I'm not leaving this time."

Later that day, Aaranya met Samuel for a walk. She didn't tell him everything—just enough.

"My house feels like walking into a memory I haven't processed yet."

Samuel nodded. "Then don't process it all at once. Grief isn't a checklist."

They paused on a bridge, watching the river flow.

"Hudson's trying," Aaranya added quietly. "I'm just not sure if I can let him in again."

"Maybe don't think of it as letting him in," Samuel said. "Maybe think of it as seeing who he's become before deciding if there's space for him."

She looked at him, grateful—not for answers, but for that steady presence beside her.

That night, Aaranya sat by her window, the chain around her neck. For the first time in a long time, she didn't feel like a stranger in her own story. There was grief, yes. But there was also something else—something new.

Maybe, just maybe, it was beginning again.

Part II: Scars (The Battle)

Chapter 6

Shadows Between Us

"Sometimes it's not the past we run from—it's the parts of ourselves that still bleed in its silence."

The days that followed felt quieter, but not peaceful. There was a strange tension hovering in Aaranya's chest, like the breath you hold just before saying something you're not sure should be said.

Samuel was still around—gentle, consistent, careful with the way he stepped into her world. And Hudson stayed too, quieter now, showing up in small ways. Fixing the creaky door. Replacing the batteries in the remote. Leaving a mug of tea beside her without asking.

Aaranya appreciated them both. But something in her felt… unsettled.

It started with a phone call.

Unknown number. A silence that stretched on the other end before a voice whispered her name and then hung up.

The kind of voice that turns blood cold.

She didn't tell anyone about it. Not Samuel. Not Hudson. She told herself it was probably a wrong number, a prank. But her body didn't believe it. Her hands trembled long after she put the phone down.

That night, she sat in her room with the lights off, staring at the gold chain around her neck.

Was she being paranoid? Or was the past beginning to knock again?

The next day, Samuel noticed the shift.

"You've been quiet," he said as they walked through the botanical garden near the outskirts of town. Spring flowers bloomed in wild abandon, but Aaranya's gaze was distant.

"I'm fine," she replied. A lie wrapped in politeness.

Samuel stopped walking. "You don't have to be."

Aaranya looked away, ashamed. "I just… sometimes I get scared for no reason."

"There's always a reason," Samuel said gently. "Even if you don't know what it is yet."

She sighed. "I got a call. Someone said my name. That's it. Nothing more. But it… it felt wrong."

Samuel's jaw tightened, but he didn't press her. "Okay. You're safe with me, you know?"

She nodded, through her eyes glistened. "I want to believe that."

"You don't have to believe it all at once," he whispered. "But I'll keep proving it until you do."

That evening, Hudson found her in the attic, sifting through old boxes.

"You always disappear up here when your mind's loud," he said, stepping carefully over a stack of photo albums.

She smiled faintly. "You still remember that?"

Hudson sat beside her. "I remember a lot more than you think."

They found an old notebook—a journal that belonged to their mother. Aaranya flipped through it slowly, the pages filled with her elegant handwriting.

"She wrote about you a lot," Hudson said. "She was proud of how you always got back up. Even when things hurt."

Aaranya blinked fast, holding back tears. "I don't feel strong."

"You don't have to," Hudson said. "Being here—facing it— that's strong enough."

That night, alone in her room, Aaranya wrote a letter to herself.

Dear Me,

It's okay to be afraid. You've been through storms people don't even know how to name. But look at you—still here, still breathing, still hoping. That's not a weakness. That's power. Let yourself rest. Let yourself feel. And when it's time, rise again.

— Love, Me

As the ink dried on the page, she didn't feel whole. Not yet. But she felt something new.

The fear hadn't left. But neither had her will to fight.

Chapter 7

Echoes of Him

"Sometimes, the people we try to forget are the ones who left fingerprints on the parts of us we never wanted touched."

Aaranya was beginning to sleep again—lightly, cautiously— but slept nonetheless. Until the nightmares returned.

Not vivid images, but feelings. The sense of being watched. The ache of helplessness. A scream lodged in her throat. And always... his voice. Not Samuel. Not Hudson. His.

She woke drenched in sweat, the chain around her neck tangled against her skin like a lifeline pulled too tight.

For days, she said nothing.

But silence has a sound, and Samuel was beginning to hear it.

One morning, while she stood in the kitchen pouring tea, he stepped beside her and asked, "Who was he, Aaranya?"

Her hand froze mid-pour. She didn't turn to face him.

"I don't want to talk about him."

Samuel didn't move. His presence was like steady rain—never forcing the storm, just quietly waiting for the flood to pass.

"I get that," he said. "But you flinch when I raise my voice. You shrink when the door creaks too loudly. You stop breathing in your sleep. If I'm going to walk this with you, I need to know what you're walking away from."

Her fingers tightened around the cup, then slowly released.

"He broke me," she said finally. "Piece by piece. With words that sounded like love. With promises that smelled like poison. And when I tried to leave, he made me believe it was my fault."

The words trembled as they escaped her. And once they were out, they refused to go back in.

Samuel didn't respond right away. He just stood there, letting her be messy, broken, honest.

"He manipulated everything," she whispered. "Made me question my worth. My sanity. He isolated me from friends, made me believe no one else would ever love me."

Samuel turned to her then, voice low and sure. "You are not what he did to you."

Later that evening, Aaranya sat by the window again, watching the rain hit the glass in rhythmic taps. Hudson appeared in the doorway, hesitant.

"I ran into someone from school today," he said casually, stepping into the room. "They asked about you. Said you used to write poems and hide them in library books."

Aaranya laughed—really laughed—for the first time in days. "That sounds like something I'd do."

"You still write?"

She nodded. "Letters mostly. To myself. Like I'm trying to remind the past version of me that we survived."

There was a pause.

Hudson's voice softened. "Did he hurt you?"

Aaranya didn't answer with words. Her silence was loud enough.

Hudson exhaled sharply, fists clenched. "I should've been there."

"You weren't," she said simply. "But you're here now. That's what matters."

That night, she found one of her old poems tucked inside a book in the attic:

I became quiet because my screams scared me.

I stayed because I thought leaving would kill me.

But now I know—

Staying was what I almost did.

She stared at the page for a long time before slipping it into her journal.

The past had begun to stir. The echoes of him were getting louder.

But this time, she wasn't alone.
And that changed everything.

Chapter 8

The Demands of Distance

"Not all distance is measured in miles. Sometimes, it's the silence between two people standing inches apart."

Los Angeles was glittering but hollow. The kind of city that smiled on the outside and ached beneath. Aaranya had thought the sunshine might help—the clear skies, the palm trees, the illusion of peace. But grief had a way of following you, no matter how far you flew from it.

Samuel could see it, even if she didn't say it out loud. The way her laughter paused too quickly. The way she looked at photographs like they were time bombs.

It was after a late dinner in their tiny LA apartment, city lights flickering beyond the windows, that he said it.

"What if we left? Just for a while. Moved to Paris."

Aaranya blinked. "Paris?"

He nodded. "You could write. I'd still work—freelance gigs, remote. Just... be somewhere else for a while. Away from the ghosts. Away from everything you're still trying to outrun."

She didn't answer right away. Her fingers traced the rim of her teacup.

"This city… it's loud," she finally whispered. "Too loud for the quiet I need."

"And yet," Samuel replied, "you've made it your cage."

That hit harder than she expected.

Later that night, they lay side by side, neither of them asleep. Samuel reached for her hand.

"You don't have to decide now," he said softly. "But if healing means putting distance between you and this city, then let's do it. Let's give you space to breathe."

"I'm scared," Aaranya admitted. "What if I run and the pain follows?"

"Then we face it together in a new place," Samuel said. "But I'd rather try that… then watch you drown here."

Two days later, he boarded a flight to Paris for a work project. Before he left, he placed a note inside her journal:

"Pain has its own language.

But so does love.

I'll be waiting in the city of light—

When you're ready to translate your silence into something whole."

Aaranya stood by the window long after his flight had taken off. LA buzzed beneath her, beautiful and broken.

Maybe it wasn't about cities.

Maybe it was about what she was finally willing to leave behind.

And what she might, someday, choose to run toward

Chapter 9

Echoes in the Quiet

"Some silences are not empty. They are full of the things we never said, and the truths we were too afraid to speak."

It had been a week since Hudson moved into the house again, and on the surface, things looked like they were healing.

They shared breakfast. They talked about mundane things—bills, repairs, old neighbours. It was easy. Almost too easy.

But ease, Aaranya had learned, could be deceptive.

She had started noticing things—little moments that unsettled her. The way Hudson always locked the back door twice. The way his smile didn't quite reach his eyes when she mentioned her therapy sessions. How he changed the subject every time their childhood came up.

One evening, while cleaning the attic, Aaranya came across an old journal—her mother's. She hadn't seen it in years. The cover was worn, the pages yellowed, the ink faded but still legible.

She hesitated, fingers trembling as she flipped through the entries.

"Hudson seems distant these days. I know he's trying, but there's something angry in him. Something I can't reach. Aaranya doesn't say much about it, but I've seen the way she flinches sometimes."

A chill passed through her.

She closed the journal quickly, breathing heavily, as if the room had shrunk. The walls felt closer. The air is thicker.

That night, when Hudson offered to cook, she watched him carefully. He was humming to himself, flipping something in the pan like nothing was wrong. Like everything was normal.

But Aaranya couldn't ignore the tightening in her chest. The quiet parts of her brain were starting to get louder. Memory—slippery, unreliable—was beginning to whisper again.

Later, when Samuel called, she stepped outside to answer.

"You sound... off," he said.

"I found something," she replied. "My mom's journal."

Samuel was quiet, letting her speak when she was ready.

"She wrote about Hudson. About how he used to be... angry. I don't remember everything. But I think... something happened. Something I buried."

Samuel's voice was gentle, steady. "Memories protect us, Aaranya. Sometimes by locking the door. But eventually, they always find a way out."

She sighed. "I'm scared."

"I know," he said. "But you don't have to do this alone."

As the night deepened, Aaranya sat by the window with the journal in his lap, Hudson laughing softly in the next room at something on TV. It was a familiar sound.

Too familiar.

But now, it didn't bring me any comfort.

It brought questions.

She stared at the journal, the weight of it pressing down on her chest. Her mind was flooded with flashes—Hudson's temper, the sharpness in his eyes, the moments where she'd felt small, unheard. She couldn't remember it all. But the pieces were coming together, and she knew, deep down, that the past wasn't as buried as she'd hoped.

As she heard Samuel's voice again through the phone, she closed her eyes, letting it anchor her.

"Samuel…" she whispered, her voice shaky, "I'm scared I'm going to lose myself again."

"You won't," Samuel reassured her softly. "Not with me. You don't have to face this alone." And in that moment, she believed him.

Chapter 10

The Memory That Never Left

"Some wounds don't scar. They remain open, just hidden beneath layers of strength, smiles, and silence."

Aaranya stood in the hallway, her fingertips grazing the frame of her childhood bedroom door. It creaked open slowly, like a scene too familiar, too rehearsed. The wallpaper was peeling, the bedspread faded. But it wasn't the room that haunted her—it was what she was starting to remember inside it.

That night, after reading her mother's journal again, something had shifted. Not just emotionally—but physically. Her body remembered. The cold. The fear. The sharpness of footsteps approaching. Hudson's voice—raised, then lowered, but always heavy with control.

She remembered being ten. Then thirteen. Then sixteen. Small things. His hand gripped her wrist too hard. The threats whispered in the dark. The gaslighting. The fear of telling anyone. And the shame that followed.

And now—years later—he had returned. With the same calm exterior, the same warm smile… but a presence that still made her flinch when he walked too close. It wasn't just in her head. The bruises that had started to appear on her arms weren't old. They were recent.

He hadn't changed.

Just evolved.

The abuse had returned. Subtle at first—grabbing her shoulder too tightly during an argument. Slamming a door when she didn't respond the way he wanted. Calling her "too sensitive." But last night, it had crossed a line.

He had shoved her.

Not hard. But hard enough to remind her of what he was capable of. Hard enough to shake her core. She had said nothing. Frozen. Then locked her bedroom door for the first time in years.

The next morning, Aaranya stood in the kitchen, Hudson pretending as though nothing had happened. "Want pancakes?" he asked, flipping them like a practiced host.

"No," she said, voice flat.

He turned, eyes narrowing slightly, just for a second. "Suit yourself."

She didn't speak again. But she felt the journal in her bag like a weapon, a truth too heavy to ignore.

Later that day, she met Samuel in a nearby garden café. She hadn't planned to tell him everything. But when he saw her wrist—red, faintly bruised—he didn't speak. He just waited.

Aaranya finally broke. "He hurt me again," she whispered. "Physically, emotionally... I don't even know when it started this time. It just crept back in."

Samuel's expression darkened, jaw tightening. But his voice remained calm. "We'll get you out of that house. Tonight."

She shook her head. "I don't want to run again. I want to face this. But not alone."

"You won't be," Samuel said, reaching across the table and taking her hand. "He doesn't control your story anymore, Aaranya. You do."

A tear slipped down her cheek. This time, it wasn't from fear—but relief. Someone finally saw her. Believed her. Stood with her.

That evening, with Samuel beside her, Aaranya began packing her things. She didn't tell Hudson. She didn't owe him that. The chain around her neck felt heavier that day—not just her mother's memory, but her own resilience anchored to it.

She would not let this repeat.

And as she walked out the door, Samuel carrying her suitcase and holding her gaze with steady, unwavering strength—she didn't look back.

Because some doors don't deserve to be reopened.

Part III: Flight (The Rise)

Chapter 11

Shelter in the Storm

"Sometimes healing doesn't begin in silence. Sometimes, it begins in the arms of someone who simply refuses to let go."

The rain came down in sheets as Aaranya stepped into Samuel's apartment that night—a quiet, warm space on the edge of Los Angeles, tucked away from the world. It wasn't grand or perfectly arranged, but it felt safe. It smelled of coffee, clean cotton, and something else she couldn't name—maybe peace.

Samuel locked the door behind them, but not out of fear. Just instinct. Protection.

He placed her bag by the couch and gently touched her shoulder. "You're safe here."

That sentence was all it took for her composure to crack. Aaranya didn't cry loudly—she just sank into him. Her forehead pressed to his chest, her body trembling with exhaustion, release, and something that felt like surrender. Not weakness—but the strength it takes to collapse in front of someone and trust they'll hold you.

Samuel didn't ask questions. He didn't offer advice. He simply wrapped his arms around her and let her fall apart.

The next morning, sunlight filtered in through the large windows, catching dust in golden streaks. Aaranya sat wrapped in one of Samuel's oversized hoodies, a cup of coffee warming her hands.

He moved quietly around the kitchen, humming a tune she didn't recognize, barefoot and half-awake—but still beautiful in that unguarded, unfiltered way.

"I hope you slept a little," he said, sliding her a plate of toast.

"I did," she said. "Because I wasn't scared."

That truth felt like a gift.

"I can find a temporary place for you to stay—if you want your space," Samuel offered.

"I don't," Aaranya said quickly, then paused. "Not yet."

He nodded, understanding. No pressure. No assumptions.

"Do you want to talk about it?" he asked.

Aaranya hesitated. "I was scared to see Hudson again. But I thought maybe he'd changed. Or maybe I'd grown stronger. Turns out, both can be true—and still, it wasn't enough to stop him from becoming what he always was."

She stared into her coffee. "He tried to control me again. But this time... I'm done hiding. I don't want to disappear into my pain anymore."

Samuel reached across the table and placed his hand over hers. "Then don't. Let it out. Every word. Every scream. Every silence. I'll be here for all of it."

Later that day, they walked to a nearby bookstore. Aaranya needed air, and Samuel knew better than to suggest isolation. The sky had cleared, leaving puddles on the pavement and the scent of rain in the wind.

Inside the bookstore, she wandered between aisles, running her fingers along spines of novels, poetry, memoirs—voices that had once felt distant. Now, she saw pieces of herself in all of them.

Samuel handed her a book—Women Who Rise. She smiled faintly.

"Too on-the-nose?" he asked with a sheepish grin.

"No," she whispered. "Perfect."

That night, they sat on the couch, her legs draped over his, the soft hum of old jazz playing from his speakers. There were no declarations. No demands. Just presence.

And then, as if time folded in on itself, he leaned in slowly— his hand cradling her cheek—and kissed her. Gently. Patiently. Like he was asking, not taking.

It wasn't rushed.

It wasn't to fill a void.

It was an answer to every question she hadn't dared to ask.

When they pulled apart, Aaranya rested her head against his shoulder.

"This isn't just shelter," she said. Samuel looked down at her, brushing a strand of hair behind her ear. "No. It's home."

Chapter 12

Where Light Finds Us

"You don't always rise from the ashes with a roar. Sometimes, you rise slowly—with trembling hands, open scars, and a quiet kind of courage."

The morning sun painted golden streaks across the hardwood floor of Samuel's apartment. Aaranya stood by the window, her fingers grazing the glass, watching Los Angeles wake up. The chaos of traffic, the blur of lives moving forward—it should've felt overwhelming. But not today.

Today, she felt still. Not empty. Just… still.

In the quiet behind her, Samuel stirred awake. His presence was steady—no demands, no pressure. Just quiet support that asked nothing in return.

She turned to him with a smile—small, but real. "Want to take a walk?"

Minutes later, they wandered through a small art district. Vibrant murals stretched across the buildings—grief in colors, joy in lines. One wall caught her eye: a woman, painted in strokes of fire and sky, arms open, eyes closed, hair turning into wings.

"She reminds me of you," Samuel said softly.

Aaranya blinked back the burn in her throat. "She looks free."

"You are," he said. "Or at least… you're becoming."

Later, they sat on a park bench beneath an oak tree. Aaranya pulled out her notebook—a habit she'd lost, but was reclaiming now. She flipped to a blank page and stared at it.

"You still write letters to yourself?" Samuel asked.

"I stopped. Because I didn't like the person I was writing to," she admitted. "But now… maybe I'm ready to start again."

She wrote:

Dear me,

You survived the fire.

Now let the light in.

When they returned to the apartment, Aaranya found a message on her phone. It was from Hudson.

"You think you're safe now? You think you can just leave everything behind and pretend I don't exist?"

She read it once. Then again. And then, without flinching, she deleted it.

"No reaction?" Samuel asked gently.

"No," she said. "He doesn't get that anymore. I've given him enough pieces of myself. I'm not handing him the rest."

That evening, Aaranya sat at Samuel's desk, surrounded by the soft hum of a jazz vinyl. She opened her journal again, and this time she wrote with intention—not just a release, but a reclaiming.

Dear Aaranya,

You are not your past. You are not what broke you. You are the girl who stood in the fire and came out glowing. You don't owe silence to your abusers. You don't owe comfort to your grief. You owe yourself freedom—and that begins now.

As the sky faded to dusk, Aaranya stepped onto the balcony, wrapped in Samuel's hoodie. He joined her quietly.

"I'm going to tell my therapist everything," she said. "No more filters. I want to face it all."

He didn't respond with encouragement or praise. He just stood beside her, his pinky brushing hers. Quiet solidarity.

For the first time in years, Aaranya felt like her voice mattered. Like her story—no matter how cracked or painful—deserved to be told. Not hidden. Not buried.

And in that moment, beneath a sky turning indigo, she finally believed—

The light had found her

Chapter 13

Letters to the Girl I Was

"Healing isn't about forgetting who you were. It's about forgiving her, loving her, and choosing who you'll become—every single day."

The therapist's office was warm, not sterile. There were soft cushions, plants by the windows, and a faint scent of lavender in the air. Aaranya sat with her palms on her lap, the journal open beside her, heart thudding.

"I want to talk about Hudson," she said.

The words left her mouth like glass—shards she was no longer afraid to hold.

For the next hour, she unraveled the tightly wound threads. The emotional manipulation, the controlling behavior that had begun long before her mother passed. The nights when he'd barged into her room shouting. The moments he'd grabbed her wrist too tightly. The times he'd made her question her own memory— "That didn't happen," "You're too sensitive," "Why do you always play the victim?"

And now, the messages. The veiled threats. The push to keep her close, to control her again.

Her therapist didn't interrupt, just listened with the kind of stillness that made Aaranya feel heard in the places she never had been.

When she finally stopped speaking, her hands were trembling—but her voice wasn't.

"I thought it was normal," she whispered. "To be treated like that. I thought… maybe I deserved it."

The therapist leaned in gently. "And what do you think now?"

"I think… I was just a girl," Aaranya said. "A scared, grieving girl. And no one protected her—not even me. But I want to know."

That night, she sat by the window with her journal. The city buzzed below, but inside was quiet.

She began to write.

Dear girl I used to be,

You were never too much.

You were never too dramatic, too emotional, too complicated.

You were hurt. And you survived. That is not a weakness. That is strength.

I'm sorry I silenced you. I'm sorry I let others define your worth.

I see you now. I believe you.

And I will never let anyone shame you into silence again.

With love,

The woman you're becoming

When Samuel came in, he didn't speak—just walked over and kissed her forehead.

"You okay?"

"I think I'm learning how to be," she said. "It's not easy. But it's real."

He sat beside her, pulling her into a loose embrace. "You're brave, Aaranya. Even when you don't feel it."

She rested her head on his shoulder, letting herself exhale.

There were still chapters left to live. Still court hearings to prepare for. Still conversations that would be hard and memories that might visit uninvited.

But there was also this: a woman, no longer hiding from her past. A heart learning how to stay open. A story finally being told—by the one who lived it.

And tonight, in a room filled with silence, strength, and second chances, Aaranya wrote one more line: I'm not who I was. I'm becoming who I was always meant to be.

Chapter 14

The Trial of Truths

"Sometimes, standing for yourself feels like standing alone. But in that solitude, truth finds its loudest voice."

The courtroom wasn't as grand as Aaranya imagined. It was smaller, colder. The lights were too bright, the benches too hard. But what unsettled her most wasn't the space—it was the silence that fell when she entered.

Samuel squeezed her hand as they sat in the gallery. His presence was quiet but grounding, like a lighthouse when the waves threatened to pull her under.

Hudson sat a few rows ahead with his lawyer, wearing a grey suit and a face he had worn many times before—the charming, polished, composed one. But Aaranya could see it now, see through it.

He didn't intimidate her anymore. He infuriated her. Not because of what he did—but because he thought she wouldn't fight.

But she was here.

The judge entered. Proceedings began. There were formalities, statements, and protocols. But when her name was called, it all faded into a single heartbeat.

She stood. Walked. Sat in the witness chair.

And spoke.

"I used to think silence kept me safe," Aaranya began, her voice steady despite the tremor in her spine. "But silence let the wrong story win."

Her statement wasn't filled with rage. It was filled with clarity. She spoke about the manipulation, the emotional abuse, the patterns that began when she was just a child and had followed her into adulthood. She shared how he'd re-entered her life only to start that cycle again—this time, more calculated, more entitled, more dangerous.

She spoke of her mother. Of the gold chain. Of the journal that unearthed memories buried deep.

On the night Hudson cornered her in the kitchen and grabbed her arm so tightly it left a bruise. Of the messages laced with guilt and gaslighting. Of how he still tried to wear the mask of a savior while being the storm.

And then she looked at the judge—not begging, not pleading, just resolute.

"I'm not asking for punishment," she said. "I'm asking for protection. For truth to be acknowledged. And for him to never have the power to rewrite my story again."

The silence that followed was not hollow. It was full. Heavy. Real.

When Aaranya stepped down, her legs felt shaky, but her spirit stood tall. Samuel met her outside the courtroom, pulling her into an embrace that needed no words.

"You did it," he whispered.

She nodded. "I finally said it all out loud."

The case was still in process, but something had already changed.

That night, Aaranya and Samuel sat on the rooftop of their small apartment in Los Angeles, wrapped in a blanket, watching the city lights.

"You were brilliant," Samuel said.

"No," Aaranya replied, leaning her head on his shoulder. "I was finally… me."

The wind picked up, carrying away the weight of old ghosts. The stars above shimmered quietly—like they, too, had been waiting for her to arrive here.

Chapter 15

Âme Libre (A Free Soul)

"Healing doesn't mean the scars disappear. It means they no longer control the way you walk."

The trial was over. Hudson was ordered to stay away—permanently. There was no spectacle in the ending, no dramatic courtroom gasp. Just quiet closure. And perhaps that was the most powerful thing of all.

Aaranya stood outside the courthouse, her hair gently tousled by the breeze, the sky above vast and open. She didn't cry. Not this time. Instead, she smiled—small, real. Because this moment wasn't about what she had survived. It was about who she had become.

It was spring in Los Angeles. The city pulsed with warmth, and everything seemed to be in bloom, even her.

Aaranya had moved out of the old apartment and into a little place near the hills. It wasn't much, but it had sunlight, bookshelves, and quiet mornings where she could hear her own thoughts without fear interrupting.

Samuel visited often. He never rushed her, never asked for more than she was ready to give. They made pancakes on Sundays, planted succulents on the balcony, and sometimes just sat in silence, fingers intertwined, hearts speaking in their own rhythm. He was in love. Not the kind that crashes in like a storm, but the kind that waits outside the door until you're ready to open it.

One morning, Aaranya sat on her writing desk, reading over her latest letter—to herself.

Dear Me,

You walked through fire and kept walking. You loved, lost, and lived through things no one should. But you are not broken. You are art built from ruin. You are softness carved from storms. And now—now, you are free.

Never forget that.

Love,

Me

She sealed the letter and placed it with the others—a box full of healing, one page at a time.

Later that week, Samuel surprised her with tickets.

"To where?" she asked.

"You've always wanted to see the northern lights, right?"

Her heart leapt. "You remembered?"

"I remember everything you say when you're not trying to be brave," he whispered.

And so, they packed light. They flew north. And one night, wrapped in layers and laughter, they stood beneath a sky painted with dancing green and purple. Aaranya looked up, eyes wide, soul still.

"This feels unreal," she whispered.

Samuel kissed her forehead. "No. This is real. You are real. And you're finally living it."

She didn't know what tomorrow would bring. But for the first time in years, she wasn't afraid of tomorrow. Because the past no longer had its grip. And the future—well, it was hers to shape now.

Aaranya wasn't the same girl who once fell in love and shattered quietly. She was something stronger. Softer. Wilder.

She was Âme Libre. A free soul.

And her story had only just begun.

To be continued....

Author's Note – For the One Who Stayed Until the End

If you're still here… thank you.

Not just for reading this story, but for holding space for every scar, every silence, and every scream that never made it to the surface.

This wasn't just a novel.

It was a burial. A resurrection. A love letter to every version of myself I once lost chasing someone else.

If you saw yourself in Aaranya, I want you to know:

You are not broken.

You are becoming.

Your softness is not your weakness.

Your survival is not your shame.

And your story — however messy, loud, or unfinished — is still yours to write.

You don't need someone to choose you to prove you are worthy.

You are already everything you've ever needed.

And if no one ever told you:

I am so proud of you for continuing.

Even, especially when it hurts.

With all my love,

– Harmanpreet Kaur

About the Author

Harmanpreet Kaur is a passionate writer and poet at heart, and a fierce believer in the healing power of words. Born and raised in Punjab, she finds inspiration in the quiet moments of life—the ache of memory, the pulse of hope, and the strength it takes to rise after a fall. Her writing often explores the depth of human emotion, the scars we carry, and the quiet resilience of those who choose to love again.

Once She Loved: Âme Libre is her debut novel—an intensely personal, emotionally charged journey through trauma, healing, and the rediscovery of self-worth. Harmanpreet writes not just to tell a story, but to make her readers feel seen, understood, and a little less alone.

When she's not writing, she enjoys long walks, stargazing, and collecting quotes that feel like home.